3 1994 01479 2557

7|12

SANTA ANA PUBLIC LIBRARY

D0388898

Troll Hunters is published by Stone Arch Books
A Capstone Imprint
1710 Roe Crest Dr.
North Mankato, Minnesota 56003
www.capstonepub.com

Copyright © 2012 by Stone Arch Books. All rights reserved. No part of this publication may be reproduced
in whole or in part, or stored in a retrieval system, or transmitted in any form or by any means, electronic,
mechanical, photocopying, recording, or otherwise, without written permission of the publisher.

Summary: A palace of nightmares rises from the ground just outside the small town of Zion Falls.
Four young heroes must prevent the dark tower from reaching the surface, or an army of pure
evil will be unleashed upon the world.

Designed by Hilary Wacholz

Cataloging-in-Publication Data is available at the Library of Congress website.
ISBN: 978-1-4342-3308-0 (library binding)

Printed in the United States of America in Stevens Point, Wisconsin.
102011
006404WZS12

Dark Tower Rising

J FICTION DAHL, M.
Dahl, Michael
Dark tower rising

$23.99
CENTRAL   31994014792557

WRITTEN BY MICHAEL DAHL

ILLUSTRATED BY BEN KOVAR

STONE ARCH BOOKS
www.stonearchbooks.com

TABLE OF CONTENTS

TO CHARLES WILLIAMS,
EMISSARY

Darkness beats his Dreadful Drums —
The Shadow comes! The Shadow comes!
Darkness cries to every Ear —
The Palaces of Night are here!
Behold the Chambers deep and dim,
Behold the Towers gaunt and grim,
Behold the Throne that carries him,
Behold the Shadow comes!

— from *Servants of the Graveyard* by
    Anthony Atwood Crake

ONE MORNING...

Bryce Gamble couldn't remember where he was. Hard ground pressed against his back. His body was cold, yet sunlight felt hot on his face. So hot that it hurt. A breeze ran over his body as strange, dark fingers seemingly reached toward him. Bryce tried to focus. The fingers slowly turned into tree branches waving high above him. Where was he? All he could remember was a battle in the darkness. Huge arms, glowing eyes, bristling fangs. Something was being hunted.

Yes. *He* had been hunting for someone last night. A little girl. But not just her. He was hunting for humans. Any humans.

He remembered being hungry for them.

1

SLIPPERY ONES

Pablo sat cross-legged in a wide, grassy field. He wasn't sure how long he'd been sitting there. It seemed like ages since he'd barely escaped the trolls.

He was still wearing his jeans and shirt from last night. His feet were still shoeless, but he felt warm. The pale October sun was just beginning to rise over the treetops.

Hroom . . . hroom . . .

Pablo shivered when he heard the noise. He turned his head, and his gaze met a pair of dark, unblinking eyes.

They bulged from mushroom-colored skin, and were as dark as a bottomless pit.

Pablo squinted against the morning light. Now he could see that the dark eyes sat atop a pale, wart-covered body about the size of a football. The football collapsed, then swelled up again. Pablo chuckled.

Just a toad, he thought. *A big one.*

Pablo pinched his eyes shut. When he opened them, he saw that there were at least a dozen of the amphibians sitting and warming themselves on a huge boulder. Mist rose from the boulder's jagged, rocky sides. A second boulder, behind the first, was also covered with the cold-blooded creatures.

Hroom . . . hroom . . . The toads were croaking deep within their throats.

It sounded like the beating of faraway drums.

Pablo knew the boulders weren't a natural part of the field. Last night, they had been living creatures, chasing him, hungry for human blood. The moon's reflected sunlight had shone down on the two trolls that had chased him and Thora, turning them into steaming rocks.

Thora, thought Pablo. *She led the trolls into the field, running like the wind. She was so running so fast last night.*

"Pablo, are you okay?" came a sleepy voice.

"Yeah," Pablo said. "Hey, look at all these frogs."

Thora groggily rose into a sitting position.

"Eww, they're everywhere!" Thora said. After a moment's pause, she added, "They sure seem to like the petrified trolls."

Pablo nodded. "Feel how warm the rocks are."

They both held out their hands as if warming themselves by a campfire. The rocks' jagged, limb-like edges gave them a frightful appearance.

"The doctor was right," Thora said. "The trolls look just like meteors from outer space when they're petrified."

Pablo glanced at the rocky shapes. "Technically, they'd be meteorites," he said. "That's what you call a meteoroid that lands on earth. A meteor is the flash of light we see when it streaks through the sky. That's what we saw last night during the meteor shower."

"Did you learn that in Mr. Thomas's science class?" Thora asked.

"I think I read it somewhere," said Pablo. "Pretty geeky, huh?"

Thora shrugged. "Not really," she lied. Standing up, stiffly, she gazed around the empty field. "I need to find my brother," she said.

Pablo turned to Thora. "Where did you last see Bryce?" he asked.

"We were all looking for Louise in the woods," she replied. "Me, Bryce, and Louise's father got separated before Dr. Hoo saved us."

Pablo remembered how he had found Zak Fisher the night before in a wrecked car. The Fishers had gotten in some weird kind of accident.

But then Zak's parents disappeared, and in the resulting search, he and Pablo had stumbled across Thora in the middle of the woods looking for a lost little girl.

"I didn't see Bryce when Zak and I found you," said Pablo.

"Bryce left his car in the middle of the road," said Thora. "That's when we all started searching for Louise. But I know he wouldn't leave me behind. Bryce has to be around here somewhere."

Pablo considered the awful size and speed of the trolls. A lone teenager wouldn't stand a chance against even one of them.

Then again, Pablo and the others had somehow managed to survive the night. Perhaps Bryce had, too.

Hrooooooom . . . hrooom . . .

One of the toads sitting on the rock opened its big mouth and yawned. It had teeth — a double row of sharp fangs that glistened with drool.

Pablo was confused. *Toads don't have teeth like that,* he thought. *What in the world are these things?*

The constant croaking started to make Pablo feel uneasy. "Uh, let's go back to the house," he said, standing up. "We should check on Zak and Louise."

"Do you think they're —" Thora began.

The sound of a strong gust of wind interrupted her. But there were no leaves moving on the nearby branches, and Pablo felt no breeze against his skin.

Thora pointed at some tall grass. "Look!" she cried.

The trees were not moving, but the grass was. It swayed in a great wave, as if an invisible hand was sweeping across the field. Pablo squinted his eyes and realized the grass was being pushed aside by something closer to the ground. And it was coming straight toward them.

"What's going on?" Pablo said, taking a step back.

Just then, countless snakes slid out from the grass. Their slithering shapes created a great river of brown and black and gray. They slid over and under each other, sunlight glistening off their scales.

"There must be thousands of them!" Thora exclaimed. "We have to get out of here!'

"Wait!" said Pablo. "They're not attacking us."

Every snake moved straight ahead, traveling toward a distant point on the horizon. "It looks like they're heading for the Nye farm," Thora said. "To the well."

Pablo knew about the well. His parents had warned him to stay away from the deep and dangerous pit ever since he was a little boy. And Dr. Hoo had said it was a secret entry point for the trolls.

Pablo stuck out a bare foot and placed it in the path of the serpents. They slid around his ankle as if it were a small tree in the path of a flood. Thora hesitated briefly, then joined him. Slowly, they made their way through the serpentine river.

"Let's go find Dr. Hoo," said Pablo. "I bet he'll know what's with all these snakes."

Thora nodded. "And he'll know how to find my brother."

2

VISITORS

A small white rental car drove through Zion Falls just before sunrise. It passed the abandoned quarry, where a heavy cloud of mist loomed over the lake. It continued past several abandoned farms and empty fields. Then it traveled by a long stretch of dark trees and into a lonely field. It pulled onto the gravel-covered shoulder, and then stopped.

Mara Lovecraft stepped out of the car. The young woman wore dark jeans, boots, and a long gray coat. Her straight black hair was tied back in a long ponytail.

She found her smart phone and checked a digital map of the area. The local homes and farms were all highlighted.

"Gamble, Tooker, O'Ryan . . . and Nye," she read.

She tapped the screen on the Nye farm and zoomed in. Then she lifted her head and stared at the far side of the field toward an old house, a few farm buildings, and a rusty silo.

"There it is," she said.

Mara looked up at the dark, early morning sky and frowned. She was sorry that she had missed the meteor shower last night. Mara heard it had been spectacular, but she had been too busy driving all night to see it. Her friend and colleague Dr. Hoo had assured her that Zion Falls would soon be the site of an even greater natural event.

Dr. Hoo said that Mara's help would be needed soon. That the future of the entire world depended on it.

Mara remote-locked the car, then stepped into the tall, wet grass. After a few minutes of walking, she had crossed only half of the field. A shiver shot through her. Mara turned up her coat collar against the cold air and continued walking. *What has Dr. Hoo gotten me into this time?* she wondered.

The ground beneath Mara's feet shuddered. She bent her head to listen. A loud moan came from directly beneath her feet. Mara smiled. She muttered a few words in a strange language toward the earth.

A moan called back to answer her. But it was not just a moan. There were words. Mara spoke again. Suddenly, the field shook fiercely as the ground rose up in front of her.

The earth moved in rippling waves. Soil, rocks, leaves, and grass heaved upward into the shape of a wall. The wall turned and twisted, its sides sloping down. Weird shapes jutted out. Shapes like legs and arms.

A breeze shuddered through the field. After the woman brushed the hair from her face, she saw a fully formed creature before her. It towered above her, like some nightmare from an ancient myth, as mud and stones and worms fell off of its limbs. The rising sun behind the woman reflected off two gleaming rocks in the figure that could easily have been mistaken for eyes.

The woman smiled. "Greetings, old friend," she said.

The shiny rocks blinked at her.

3

CALL OF THE FLIES

Zak Fisher woke up in a panic. *Mom! Dad! Where are you?!*

He threw off an unfamiliar blanket and stared up in confusion at a high, vaulted ceiling. The room was shaped like an octagon. Four of the sides were covered with floor-to-ceiling windows. Three sides were covered with tall bookshelves. A heavy door in the last wall was sealed shut.

It took a few long moments before Zak realized where he was. *Dr. Hoo's library,* he remembered.

Stiffly, Zak rose up from the sofa he had been sleeping on. He was still wearing the jeans and sweatshirt from the night before. They were dirty and torn, with several spots of dried blood on his shirt.

Is that my blood? he wondered.

Zak's memory was fuzzy, but he did remember that Dr. Hoo had saved them — Zak, Pablo, and Thora — when they were attacked in the woods. Dr. Hoo drove the three of them back to his house. To this room. They had locked the door to the library when the trolls attacked. But then Pablo and Thora had climbed out the windows to lead those monsters away.

Zak shuddered. He would never forget those unbelievable creatures. They had been inside the house, below the library, their giant hands reaching for his friend through the windows.

The doctor had told them that the trolls came from somewhere deep inside the earth to claim the planet as their own. To enslave humans. And worse.

Just then, the door pushed open with a slow creak. Zak twitched nervously.

"You're finally awake!" said a small blond girl.

Zak breathed a sigh of relief. "Louise," he said. "Where is everybody?"

"Me and Dr. Hoo are eating breakfast," she said, as if it were the most normal thing in the world. "He asked me to come check on you."

"But what about Pablo and Thora?" Zak asked. "Where are they?"

"They stopped the trolls out in the field," Louise announced proudly.

"So, they're gone?" Zak asked.

Louise nodded. She looked calm and happy and at ease. *Great,* thought Zak. *An eight-year-old is handling all of this better than I am.*

Suddenly, Louise's eyebrows shot up. She ran past Zak and pounced on the sofa.

"There you are!" she exclaimed. Nestled within the folds of Zak's blanket was a small brown and white bunny. "I looked for you all night," Louise said, nuzzling it.

She turned to Zak. "Did you find him?" she asked gleefully. "Thank you so much!" Louise hugged Zak around the shoulders. The bunny's soft ears tickled Zak's chin as she hugged him.

Zak shook his head. He felt dizzy and confused. A dull pain ached in his head. He felt blood crusted under a nostril.

"That can't be good," Zak muttered.

"The doctor said you were in a car accident," said Louise, playing with her pet.

The accident! Zak remembered. *Mom, Dad . . . I have to find them.*

"After the trolls were gone, you sat down on the sofa," said Louise. "You said you felt sleepy, so Dr. Hoo gave you a blanket. Don't you remember?"

No, he couldn't remember. A buzzing sound seemed to be slowly filling his head.

Then Louise ran to a window. "Buzz, buzz," she said.

Zak walked up next to her and looked out. The buzzing was coming from outside. Dark, glistening clouds spiraled into long funnels.

"Look at all those flies!" cried Louise.

Louise was right. The clouds were, in fact, twisting swarms of insects. Millions of them. They flew past the house to the south, following County Road One.

"Where are they going?" asked Louise.

"No idea," said Zak. He heard more buzzing. He lowered his gaze to see several large houseflies banging themselves against the glass. Zak flipped the latch and opened the window. The insects zoomed off to join the swarm.

"Cool!" cried Louise.

I think I'm gonna be sick, thought Zak.

Louise turned away from the window. Still holding on to her bunny, she grabbed one of Zak's arms with her free hand and pulled him toward the door. "Come on," she said. "You look hungry!"

4

HUNGER

From the edge of the field, Thora and Pablo could see Dr. Hoo's house. "It looks taller from this side," Thora said.

"I know," said Pablo. "It's weird, but I swear it was only two stories yesterday."

They walked along the line of trees that marked the boundary between the field and the doctor's overgrown yard. Above them, the highest tree branches blocked the sunlight from above.

Thora shivered in the shadows. She glanced around the yard, taking it all in.

The scraggly bushes next to the house reminded her of crouching trolls — like the one that had sung to her in the woods. The knobby, leafless branches looked like the arms that had reached for her.

Are the trolls really gone? she wondered.

Next to the edge of Dr. Hoo's house was a tall bush that still had most of its leaves. It stood as tall as a man and swayed gently in the breeze. There was a strange shadow on the other side of it.

Suddenly, she heard a whisper. *Thora . . . don't forget me . . .*

"What did you say?" Thora asked Pablo.

Pablo frowned. "I didn't say anything," he said. "Oh, you mean about the house?"

"No," Thora said. "Did you say something after that?"

"Nope," Pablo said, narrowing his eyes at her. "Are you feeling okay?"

The sunlight was inching farther down the branches of the trees. Soon, the sun would be creeping above the roof. But the dark and gloomy bush seemed to be growing darker and larger.

Thora . . . I'm hungry . . .

"You're hungry?" she asked Pablo.

"I guess," said Pablo. "Are you?"

I need you . . .

Thora swung her head left and right. *It's not Pablo's voice,* she realized.

It felt like whispers were coming from all around her. Cold shivers ran up and down Thora's spine. "Where's the door?" she asked, her voice cracking.

"What?" said Pablo.

Thora ran past Pablo and rushed toward the house. "The door!" Thora repeated. "The bushes are blocking the door!"

A thick barrier of intertwined branches and vines had risen between them and the front door.

"Thora, don't —!" Pablo cried. But she was already worming her way through the bushes, shoving branches aside. Twigs snapped. Vines dragged behind her, seemingly sucking her in.

Pablo pushed himself in, following her path. Vines clung to his shirt and his jeans. Pablo pulled them off hastily.

The bushes grew thicker and darker the farther they ventured. With each branch they pushed aside, more whipped back at them.

"How much farther is it?" called Pablo.

Thora put her head down and kept shoving. At one point, the branches grew so thick that they seemed to block out all light.

Thora . . . Thora . . .

No, she thought. *I won't listen to it!*

Thora's arms were scratched and bleeding, but she kept pushing forward, ripping vines from her arms and legs as she moved. Finally, she emerged on the other side, scraped and bloody. She let out a sigh of relief.

"Thora!" cried Pablo's voice. "Help!"

"Take my arm!" Thora said.

She extended her small white hand through the webbed branches. She felt a strong tug on her hand and pulled Pablo through the dark and into the light.

Pablo leaned against the wall, panting from the effort. The door stood a few feet away. "Are you okay?" he asked.

"I'm — I'm just tired," she said. "And hungry."

"Me too," said Pablo.

As Pablo closed the door behind them, Thora noticed a darker shape within the twigs and branches. It looked like a shadow that formed the outline of a person.

Thora . . . Thora . . . Thora!

"Thora?" Pablo said. She looked at Pablo and saw a silver light shining in his eyes. At that moment, the whispers stopped.

Without saying a word, Pablo led Thora into the house, toward the welcoming aroma of fried eggs and bacon.

5

Bryce Gamble

Bryce Gamble was no longer lying on the ground in the forest. Somehow, after what seemed like centuries, he had pulled away from the vines and grass. Slowly, he had crawled to the edge of the forest where he saw a house in the distance. It felt like months had passed since he'd been separated from Thora in the forest. They'd been looking for Louise, and lost sight of each other.

Food, he thought. *I must have food.*

Hunger pushed Bryce onward. He trudged closer to the house. Each step felt as if his feet had turned to rock.

He stopped to catch his breath by the corner of the house. The sun was rising higher. The light stung his face and hands. He wished he could hide from the light. Suddenly, a shadow covered his limbs. It formed around his body like a second skin, cooling him, calming him.

The darkness around him grew deeper and thicker. He felt safe and protected now. He also felt stronger.

Then Bryce heard voices. A girl and a boy, walking together, talking. They were heading toward the house. Toward him.

Thora . . .

Thora glanced around, but kept walking.

Bryce tried to call Thora's name, but his lips wouldn't move. Shadows shaped like vines were wrapped around his mouth and face, changing him . . .

Thora . . . help me . . .

Why doesn't she stop? Bryce thought. *It must be Pablo's fault. Yes, it's all his fault.*

Pablo and Thora were talking to each other. Bryce couldn't understand the words they were speaking. It sounded like another language. But Bryce knew Pablo was taking Thora away. Stealing her.

No! Bryce thought. *I won't let him!*

Now Thora was running. Bryce had to stop them. Something made him feel like it was important to prevent them from entering that house.

I'm so hungry . . .

Why don't they see me? Bryce wondered. He tried to grab them. It took all of his willpower to grasp onto Pablo's clothes and arms. The shadow clinging to Bryce made it seem like Pablo was passing right through him. The shadow surrounding him was so dark now that he could barely see at all.

Before Bryce knew it, the two had passed him. They were entering the door!

Thora, thought Bryce. *Thora . . . Thora!*

Bryce watched Pablo lead Thora inside. He slammed the door shut behind them.

A wild hatred boiled inside of Bryce. Pablo had taken Thora away. Bryce felt his hunger grow even stronger. *He must be destroyed,* Bryce thought. *I must eat.*

Like an old oak with deep roots, Bryce waited patiently for the boy to return.

Hours crawled by, but Bryce did not move. The shadow swarmed around him, keeping him safe from the dangerous sunlight. It whispered comfortable, familiar things to him.

Then Bryce realized something. *If Pablo does return, how can I stop him? It's hard for me to even move. He's so fast.*

There were others behind him. He turned, slowly, to see that the yard was filling up with other shadows. Other people. Or were they simply more bushes that he hadn't noticed before?

He saw dark, shadowy forms within the bushes. Several men, a woman, a child. The shadows slithered and shifted. Bryce couldn't see their faces, but he knew they were his friends. They would wait with him.

They would help him.

6

Rusty silo

Mara walked confidently across the field. Following close behind her, like a crooked shadow, was the hulking troll. It lumbered heavily through the tall grass as they approached the Nye farm. As they neared the house, Mara noticed its peeling paint, missing roof shingles, and broken windows.

It looks abandoned, Mara thought. Still, she walked up to the front door and knocked. Uzhk, her troll companion, stood silently behind her.

After no one answered, Mara knocked again. "Hello," she called. "Anyone there?"

No response came. "Hello," Mara said once more. "I'm Mara Lovecraft. We spoke on the phone last week."

Mara put her face up to the door's window and peered in. "What a mess," she mumbled to her companion. "I don't know how anyone lives out here in the middle of nowhere."

A grunt escaped the creature's lips.

Mara walked to the rear of the house. She saw an SUV sitting in the driveway that curved up behind the house. The front end was smashed in. The hood was missing and the windshield was shattered. Two of the tires were missing. But what made Mara shiver were the deep scratches along one side of the car.

Scratches made by gigantic claws.

"Do you think someone's been here recently, Uzhk?" she asked, looking over her shoulder. The creature slowly nodded.

Mara approached the car. There were gouges in the dirt behind the vehicle. *Something dragged it to this spot,* she realized. In front of the car was more of the tall, dry grass. *No tow truck brought the car here,* Mara thought. *Otherwise, there would be tracks from the truck leading through the grass.*

"Come on," Mara said, motioning for Uzhk to follow.

The strange companions headed toward a large, rusty silo in the distance. A moment later, Uzhk reached out a massive hand and touched Mara's shoulder.

"What is it?" Mara asked.

The creature cocked its head as if it were listening to a distant sound. Mara nodded. She heard it now, too — a sound like a strong breeze. But when she looked back at the trees, she saw that there was no wind.

But next to the house, the grass weeds bent low, creating a channel that headed directly toward her. The overgrown yard looked like a quiet lagoon with an invisible alligator swimming through it.

"*Thyul hu,*" growled Uzhk.

"Snakes," Mara agreed.

A river of shiny scales and darting tongues emerged into the open. Mara hopped onto the rear fender of the wrecked car. The troll looked amused by the countless snakes that swarmed around his feet.

Something vaguely resembling a smile appeared on Uzhk's face. Mara had read that trolls couldn't smile. It had something to do with the anatomy of their skulls.

Of course, Uzhk was a *drakhool*, different from the larger, more ruthless *gathool*. The two species of trolls were natural enemies. The *drakhool* believed in leaving humans alone — not in enslaving or eating them.

The reptiles continued to move, ignoring Mara and Uzhk. All of them moved with a single mind, like a net of living ropes gliding across the grass. Mara saw they were heading to the same destination: the silo.

Mara leapt off the car and followed them. She and Uzhk ran to the curving wall of the rusted tower. The serpents rushed forward, hurling themselves through the door and into the dark pit inside.

Uzhk bent down, preparing to follow the slithering horde down into the chasm. Mara stopped him, shaking her head. "We need help," she said.

The young woman pulled her phone from a pocket. *If Dr. Hoo was right,* she thought, *then we'll need a lot of help.*

Uzkh suddenly groaned, putting his hands to his ears as a monstrous hiss echoed through the silo. A vast number of serpent throats sounded a collective cry from deep down in the pit. Mara couldn't tell whether the snakes were frightened or overjoyed, but something had surprised them inside that building.

And Mara had a terrible feeling that she knew what it was.

7

STARDUST

After breakfast, Dr. Hoo led Thora, Pablo, Zak, and Louise back upstairs to the library. "There's something all of you must see," he said.

Dr. Hoo burst through the door at the top of the stairs and hurried to the center of his library. White clouds and blue sky greeted them through all four windows. Sunlight streamed across the floor and lit up a wooden stand. A large book on top was already open. Dr. Hoo approached it and flipped through pages. "We'll find what we need in here," he said.

The yellowing pages were covered with colorful paintings of stars and comets and constellations. One painting showed a half-horse, half-man holding a bow and arrow.

"That looks like the centaur we saw in the woods!" said Pablo.

Dr. Hoo looked at him and grinned. "Exactly," he said. "He's also known as Sagittarius." He turned the page, revealing two young men standing side by side. They held long swords in their hands.

"That's the Gemini constellation," said Thora, tilting her head. "We learned about the zodiac in astronomy class."

The doctor turned the page again. The next painting showed a beautiful woman wearing a crown. She held a large stone jar above her head. A strange liquid poured out from it like a brilliant shower of stars.

"Aquarius?" asked Thora. "But I thought it was supposed to be a man."

"Not always," said the doctor. "It is said that the water in her magical cup can preserve life, or snuff it out."

"She's pretty," whispered Louise.

Zak threw his hands up. "What's the deal?" he asked. "Why are we looking at pictures of some stupid stars?"

"They're more than just stars," said Dr. Hoo. "Just as the legends about trolls are real, so are the legends behind the constellations."

"What do you mean?" asked Thora. "How is any of this going to help us?"

"Be patient," Dr. Hoo scolded, turning another page. "You'll have your answers shortly."

The next page's constellation was a huge serpent. Its long body was coiled in seven silver knots.

"The Draco constellation," Dr. Hoo said. "The meteor shower last night was called the Draconid shower, because it looked like the meteors came from Draco."

The doctor flipped another page. It showed the silhouette of a ferocious beast traced against a backdrop of stars.

"A bear!" cried Louise.

"The Great Bear," Dr. Hoo said. He looked across the book toward Zak. "Also known as Ursa Major."

The doctor turned one more page. It showed a painting of a young, bearded warrior holding a club in one hand and a lion's head in the other.

"Orion," Pablo said without hesitation. Dr. Hoo nodded at him.

"We're wasting time," growled Zak. "We need to find my parents."

"And my brother," Thora added, crossing her arms.

"I understand," Dr. Hoo said, "but there's more. The legends of many ancient peoples tell of a huge battle. A war between the powers of darkness and the powers of light. Many ancient texts tell the story of an ancient dragon who fought with the stars in the sky."

Thora's eyes brightened. "Falling stars?" she repeated. "You know, at the meteor shower . . . I swear I saw a star fall from Orion's belt."

"Perhaps you did," the doctor answered.

Dr. Hoo leaned closer to the others. "Perhaps the ancient stories describe a real, true war," he suggested. "A war between a creature of darkness and beings of light. That battle may still be going on. And the trolls, emerging from deep below the surface, may have begun a new war."

Silence swept over the room, each person lost in thought. Wind rattled the library windows. Moving trees threw shadows across the ancient pages of the book.

Zak finally broke the silence. "That doesn't help me find my mom and dad," he said. "Where are they, Doc?"

Dr. Hoo stared down at the desk. "I'm not sure," he said. "But I know that by defeating these creatures, we stand a better chance of finding your parents. And your brother, Thora."

Thora squinted. "If everything you're saying is true," she said, "then how can the stars help us?"

Dr. Hoo grinned. He opened his mouth to speak, but just then, a few musical notes chimed out. The doctor pulled his phone from beneath his cape. As he moved away and spoke in hushed tones, the rest of them leafed through the book.

Zak rubbed his forehead, visibly upset. "These star things, these constellations," he said. "Is he trying to tell us they're, like, real people? That they're on Earth right now?"

"Stars aren't people," Thora said sternly. "They're gigantic balls of gas and chemicals. The closest star is light-years away. Even if someone could travel at the speed of light, it would take years to get here."

"Are you sure about that?" Dr. Hoo said. He clicked his phone shut and returned it to the folds of his cape. "The entire universe is made of the same basic matter, the same atoms. All of us were originally made from stardust."

Dr. Hoo walked back to the book. He placed his hands on the volume, turning one last page as he spoke. "Perhaps the old astrologers were trying, in a superstitious way, to explain the connection between us and the stars," he said. "After all, what earlier people used to call magic was eventually known as science. Lightning wasn't a magical weapon thrown by Zeus — it was electricity."

No one spoke for a moment. Everyone, even the doctor, seemed to be lost in their thoughts — and in the pages of the book.

After a moment, Louise piped up. "Who was on the phone?" she asked.

"That was a colleague of mine," said the doctor. He pointed at the broad shelf behind him. "She's the one who gave me those books about the *gathool* that I showed you last night. And now she needs our help."

Zak's eyes narrowed. "What kind of help?"

"She's found where the trolls are planning to attack next," said the doctor. "And if we can't stop them, all of Zion Falls will be destroyed."

8

Oɴ ᴛʜᴇ Rᴏᴀᴅ

Dr. Hoo hurried Thora, Louise, Zak, and Pablo down a long passageway that ended in a heavy metal door. He opened seven different locks.

"Why don't we just go out the front door?" asked Pablo.

"The other entrance is . . . too dangerous right now," the doctor said.

Dr. Hoo pulled the door open with a powerful tug. His SUV was parked a few feet away.

As they all left the building, Dr. Hoo reached inside his cape and pulled out a set of keys. He tossed them to Zak, who nimbly caught them.

"Do any of you know where the old Nye farm is?" Dr. Hoo asked. "The one with the big silo?"

"I know where it is," said Pablo.

"Good," said the doctor. "Show Zak how to get there."

Dr. Hoo opened the SUV's rear door and ushered Louise and Thora inside. "Please hurry," Dr. Hoo said. "Mara needs your help. It should only take you a few minutes to get there."

"Aren't you coming with us?" asked Thora.

The doctor didn't answer.

Dr. Hoo stared back at the trees and bushes surrounding his house. Although the sun had risen higher, the shadows were deeper around the old stone building.

The doctor turned back to them. Pablo looked intently at his swirling cape. Although Pablo still couldn't see within the cape's shadows, he was certain that he saw something move beneath its folds. A third arm.

"Mara's waiting for you," Dr. Hoo said. "Now hurry. I'll be there as soon as I can."

Zak roared the engine to life. As the doctor waved goodbye, the SUV bounced down the dirt driveway. A moment later, they turned east onto County Road One.

A few moments later, Pablo pointed out a dirt path up ahead. "That's the road to the Nye farm," he told Zak.

Zak stomped on the accelerator. The SUV zoomed right past the dirt path.

"Zak, where are you going?" asked Thora. "Turn around — right now!"

"Hold on," said Zak. "I need to do something first."

A few miles down the road, Zak finally hit the brakes. There, in the center of the road, the pieces of a car were scattered on the asphalt. Two tires lay on their sides. A crumbled, detached hood rested between them. The remains of a windshield were scattered across the road from one side to the other.

Zak jumped out of the SUV. "It's gone," he said softly.

Pablo turned to Thora and Louise in the back seat.

"This is where Zak's family had the accident," Pablo explained. "I saw the car. It was right there."

Pablo, Thora, and Louise all climbed out of the car. Slowly, they walked toward Zak.

"Maybe they towed it away," said Thora.

Pablo shook his head. "Then why did they leave all this junk here?" he asked.

Zak stared at the scattered glass and debris. "Someone took it," he said. "Some *thing* took the whole car!"

Louise pulled her rabbit closer. "The big bad wolf," she whispered.

"Let's get back in the car, Zak," Pablo suggested. "I think the doctor was right — if we help his friend Mara stop these trolls, then we'll be able to find your folks."

"And Bryce," added Thora.

Zak spun to fast them. "Us? *Help?*" he growled. "This is a job for the cops, the National Guard, or something!"

Pablo faced the open road and spread his arms out. "Look at the road," he said. "Do any of you see anything weird?"

"You mean besides my dad's missing car?" said Zak angrily.

"The accident was last night," said Pablo. "We've been gone for, what, 18 hours? So why didn't anyone else move this debris? It covers the entire road."

"So?" asked Thora.

"So," said Pablo, "that means no one has traveled on this road since then. Where are the police? What about people driving to school, or to work? And listen to how quiet it is."

Everyone craned their necks to listen. Not one bird sang. Not a single horsefly hummed. All the sounds of a normal October afternoon were missing.

"We might not be the only ones who came across trolls last night," Pablo added.

Pablo's comment made Thora glance nervously at the nearby trees. "Get in the car, Louise," she said, leading the girl by the shoulder.

"Yeah," agreed Pablo. "Let's get out of here."

Zak shook his head. His dark hair hung in front of his downcast face.

"Zak," Pablo said. "The doctor gave you the keys. He's counting on us. His friend needs our help."

Zak let out a deep sigh.

Zak looked over at Pablo, then straightened up with a jerk.

"Pablo," Zak said, "your eyes look . . . weird."

"What? Mine?" said Pablo.

"Yeah," said Zak. "Shiny. Like stars. You're not going to turn into a zombie or something, are you?"

Pablo grinned. "We're hunting trolls, not zombies."

Zak smirked. "Oh yeah. What was I thinking?" he said. "Zombies aren't real."

Everyone laughed — except Thora. Her face was as white as a sheet. She lifted a finger to point behind the others.

When they turned, they saw the entire SUV was crawling with giant, croaking toads.

9

SHADOWS

As the SUV disappeared down his gravel driveway, Dr. Hoo felt a cold shadow envelop his body. But unlike most October shadows that came down from above, this shadow came up from below. A strange gray mist was seeping out of the ground.

The doctor had been waiting for this to happen. The natural surroundings were being affected by the trolls' return to the surface. Vegetation, animal life, even the weather — they were all beginning to fall under the control of the *gathool*, under the growing influence of their evil presence.

Icy coldness grasped the doctor's feet. It crawled up his legs. Mist swirled around his body like a creeping vine.

Dr. Hoo closed his eyes and concentrated. Being frightened by the dark mist would only make it harder to resist. Instead, the doctor thought about the young heroes in his SUV. They would eventually need his help. He had to be strong for them.

Slowly, he pulled his left foot off the ground. Then his right. It felt like he was walking through thick mud. Each and every step took great effort.

When Dr. Hoo finally reached his house, his shirt was soaked in sweat. He shut the door behind him and turned all seven locks. Then he pressed his face to the small-paned window.

He saw bushes flailing back and forth outside. But there had been no wind when he was outside.

Dr. Hoo started down the passageway back to his library, his head hung low from exhaustion. Weakened, he slowly trudged up the stairs. As he entered the library, he heard a gravelly voice.

"Doctor?"

Dr. Hoo raised his gaze to see a young man blocking his path. Wet leaves clung to his clothes and his uncombed hair. His eyes glittered darkly behind a pair of cracked glasses. The boy was completely still, except for his twitching fingers at the ends of his long, skinny arms.

"Bryce?" Dr. Hoo asked uncertainly. "Is that you?"

The boy clenched his fists. Dr. Hoo saw that he held a pocket knife in one of them.

"Doctor," the young man repeated, his voice cold and hard. "Where is Thora?"

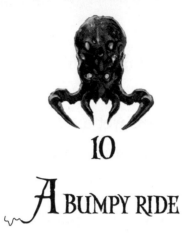

10

A BUMPY RIDE

"Gun it, Zak!" yelled Pablo.

"I can't see the road!" Zak cried. He flipped on the windshield wipers, but they couldn't move the squat, sticky bodies of the countless toads.

"Just turn us around!" said Pablo.

Zak slammed the SUV into reverse. The tires squealed against the asphalt as the vehicle whipped to the side. The sickening splats of squished toads sounded from below their seats.

"Yuck," said Louise.

The SUV raced down the road, but the view was still blocked. Zak looked out the window. Countless wet toads were slapping softly onto the asphalt all around the vehicle.

"They're falling from the sky!" Thora cried out.

"Hold on!" yelled Zak. He swerved the SUV back and forth. The movement rocked his passengers from side to side, but it also flipped some of the toads off the front of the vehicle.

"The turn isn't that far from here," Pablo announced.

Five more fat toads plopped onto the windshield. Zak spun the steering wheel back and forth, jerking the SUV around violently. Louise screamed.

"Why did we bring her?" asked Zak. "We should have taken her home."

"I don't have a home," whimpered Louise.

"It burned down," added Thora.

Zak frowned. "I'm sorry," he said, "but she's just a child. She might get hurt."

Louise pulled herself up and leaned over the front seat. "I can help," she said. "I hit that one troll with my flare gun." To make her point, she pulled the flare pistol from her nightgown pocket and waved it confidently in Zak's face.

"She *did* save Thora," said Pablo. "That troll might have gotten her."

Zak clenched his teeth. "Okay, okay," he said. "Just don't let her fire that thing in here."

Louise plopped back down next to Thora in the back seat. "I'm not a child," Louise muttered. Thora chuckled and pulled the girl close.

"There's the road!" yelled Pablo.

Zak gripped the wheel and made a hard left. The SUV flew off the asphalt and onto a dusty dirt road. The bumps and ruts threw several more toads off the vehicle. Only a few still managed to cling to the hood as the vehicle bounced wildly over the bumpy terrain.

Pablo pointed his shaking arm toward the front of the car. "I can see the Nye farm up ahead," he said.

A moment later, the SUV squealed to a halt next to the old house. "That's my parents' car," Zak said grimly. "What's it doing here?"

11

THE DARK TOWER

Everyone piled out of the SUV and raced over to Zak's parents' car. Zak ran his fingers along the deep scratches along the sides. He looked up, dazed, at Pablo. "Trolls?" he asked.

Pablo nodded grimly.

"Over here!" came a voice from behind. A young woman jogged up to greet them. She wore dark jeans tucked into a pair of muddy boots. A black ponytail hung over the collar of her long gray coat.

"I'm Mara Lovecraft," she said. "The doctor sent you, right?"

Thora nodded. "But I don't know how we can help you."

"I have a flare gun," said Louise, holding up her weapon.

Mara looked down at the little girl, a confused look on her face.

"The doctor said you figured out where the trolls were going to attack next," said Pablo.

Mara's face lit up with surprise. "Orion," she said.

Pablo squinted. "O'Ryan? How did you know my last name?" he asked.

"Last name?" said Mara. "I don't. I mean, I . . . didn't the doctor tell you?"

Zak took a step forward. "Tell us what?" he demanded.

"I've been trying to call him," Mara said, "but he isn't answering his phone. It's not like him to ignore calls."

"What was the doctor supposed to tell us?" Zak repeated.

"How you can help," Mara said. "How all of you can help. Hurry, come with me!"

Mara led them to the rusty silo. A huge gaping hole had been ripped in its side. Hundreds of toads and frogs were hurling themselves through the doorway and into the dark pit inside. A loud hissing sound echoed inside the silo.

"What's with all these creatures?!" cried Zak. "There must be thousands of them!"

"The trolls — the *gathool* — are entering our world," said Mara. "They are sending up their own ship from deep within the earth."

"What kind of ship?" asked Thora.

"It's called the *bazhargak*, or Dark Tower," said Mara. "The best way to describe it is a moving castle. A huge building filled with hundreds of *gathool*. That's why the reptiles and amphibians — their servants — are here. They've come to help the tower rise to the surface."

A tremor shook the ground.

"It's coming!" said Mara. "The Dark Tower's highest point will pierce through the ground and rise up through this silo. The *gathool* picked this site so no one would see them arrive . . . until it was too late."

Another tremor ran through the farmyard. A loud metallic shriek sounded from deep within the silo.

"Can it be stopped?" asked Pablo.

Mara shook her head weakly. "I don't know."

"Then why did the doctor send us here?" Zak yelled. "What's this got to do with getting my parents back? Why isn't Dr. Hoo here to help?!"

A harsh groan forced them all to look upward. The silo was swaying, tilting, and grinding against its cement foundation. Zak walked up next to the pit and stared deep down into the blackness. "I see it!"

The others crept closer to the edge of the pit. The, wide rounded tunnel plunged straight into the heart of the earth.

A few hundred feet below lay a slick green bulb. It reminded Thora of a gigantic acorn squash. Except this squash was a hundred times larger and had pale green spikes growing from the center. Slimy black tentacles waved around its sides. They were covered with red suckers that shone wetly in the dim light. It was rising quickly.

"That's only the tip of the tower," Mara said. "The entry gate is near the bottom. That's where the troll army will exit. If that happens . . . our world is doomed."

Suddenly, the top of the green squash split open like a pus-filled wound. A dark figure forced its way up, climbing through the slimy mass. He perched himself atop of the rising shape, his gigantic muscles tensed, preparing for battle.

"A troll!" shouted Zak. "A big one!"

"The doctor should be here," whispered Mara.

Suddenly, a dark cloud rose from the fields and surrounded the silo like a thick, black curtain hovering in the air. Then, with alarming speed, darkness surrounded them on all sides.

Everything went black.

12

LORDS OF THE FLIES

Flies. Countless flies.

They swarmed around the silo, circling like a tornado made of insect wings and night. Flies buzzed in their ears, crawled in their hair, and swept across their eyes.

"The flies are blocking out the light!" Mara cried. "I can't see anything!"

"We have to stop —" Pablo began, then he gagged. He spat out a mouthful of insects. "We have to stop them!"

More tremors rocked the earth. The silo's metal partially tore away from the concrete base. Louise dropped her rabbit. It scooted away and disappeared into the furious swarm.

Pablo's mind raced. Blurred thoughts came quickly. *How?* he thought. *How can we do anything?* He and Thora had come up with a plan to outrun the trolls last night. But they couldn't run from this.

Dr. Hoo had said that the stories of the warrior constellations were real. *As real as trolls,* Pablo remembered. *But if that's true, then where are they now?*

Pablo tried to think of a solution. He knew that sunlight would destroy a troll, but even though an afternoon sun blazed somewhere in the sky, the curtain of flies was creating its own nighttime.

They were shielding the monstrous troll at the tip of the tower from the damaging sunlight.

For some reason, Pablo recalled the starlight he saw in Zak's eyes earlier. Zak had said Pablo's eyes shone, too. *Are we really warriors from the stars?* Pablo thought. It was all jumbled up in his head. Starlight. Constellations. Magic. Science.

Pablo heard the roaring grow louder in his left ear. But the sound was different now. It was deeper, like a growl. He opened his eyes and almost screamed. Pablo had expected to see Zak standing next to him. Instead, a giant silver bear was growling wildly at the insect swarm!

It raised its thick, furry arm above its head. Pablo couldn't believe his eyes as the tremendous, hairy paw swiped at the flies.

With each sweep of its massive arm, hundreds of flies fell lifelessly to the ground. Not only the bear's swipes, but its silver light also seemed to be damaging the buzzing swarm.

It's Zak! Pablo realized.

Pablo called out to the bear, but his voice sounded deeper. Older. He looked down and saw huge weapons in his hands. Then he saw that his clothes had changed. An ornate metal breastplate covered his chest. A thick kilt of leather strips protected his thighs. His feet were no longer bare, either. Instead, he was wearing sandals. He was dressed like an ancient Roman warrior!

Pablo instinctively swung his weapons back and forth, spilling silver light along the arc of his weapons' paths. Flies fell by the hundreds at each blow.

Pablo and the silver bear fought side by side. Their brilliant light radiated into the swarm, burning away at its center.

Where are Thora and Louise? Pablo wondered. He turned to his right and saw two young women dressed in flowing silver robes. They resembled his two friends, but they also looked like the zodiac images in Dr. Hoo's book. The taller girl was trying to lift an ornate jar of gleaming light off of the ground. The jar vibrated with energy. She lifted with all her might, but couldn't lift the jar past her waist. Her arms shook as she tried to raise it above her head.

"I can't lift it!" Thora's voice cried out from the woman's lips. "It's too heavy!"

Louise stepped forward. She reached up and braced the jar with her small, silver hand. It immediately glowed brighter.

Up and up, Louise helped Thora lift it. Slowly but surely, they lifted the jar over Thora's head.

Suddenly, a flood of molten silver gushed out of the jar like water out of a burst dam. Wave after wave spilled into the pit, beating down against the rising tower. The brilliant liquid streamed impossibly from the jar without slowing. Its flow also splashed against the swarming insects, pushing them back.

The hunter and the bear kept batting at the flies. The insects fell at their sandaled or hairy feet. Thora and Louise kept the jar held high. Soon, the flood had filled most of the deep tunnel with a silvery liquid. The slimy green top of the tower sat just above the water level, like a rotten lily pad on a silver pond. It was still rising.

Pablo could see the troll at the tip of the tower. He was only a few hundred feet from the surface now. The troll braced himself against the flood, managing to hang on despite its rushing force.

But the tower continued to rise. Its black tentacles waved furiously as they pulled the tower closer and closer to the surface.

Then the earth began to tremble. This time, it wasn't the Dark Tower that shook the ground. The women's jar was gleaming brighter and brighter. It blazed like a small, silver-white star.

"It's too hot!" shouted Thora.

"Don't worry," came Louise's voice. "I can help." She touched the jar with her silver hand again. The gleaming light began to flow out of the jar!

Small stars began to surge out from the jar. They filled the silo with brilliant light. One shooting star struck the troll and knocked him off the tower.

The monster tumbled down, down, disappearing into the shining, silver lake.

"YES!" cried Thora.

But soaring through the flame and smoke, the evil tower still rose. Thora choked and coughed on the bitter fumes.

"Don't stop now!" cried Louise's voice.

The groaning in the silo grew louder. The ground shook. The insect swarm tightened its circle around the companions. But the fiery stream kept pouring from the jar, and the two warriors kept up their attack.

Thora heard a screech echo within the metal silo.

It grew loud as thunder, then suddenly faded as the stampede of flies rushed away.

Something was happening to the tower. Its circle of tentacles, blackened and charred, no longer waved. The tower's ascent was slowing.

The four warriors gasped as the tower slowly creaked its way up past the surface. Then it came to a stop as the tip of the tower scraped against the roof of the silo. At once, the starlight that had surrounded the warriors faded, and their bodies changed back to their normal forms.

Suddenly, a ball of flame formed at the tip of the tower. "Get back!" shouted Mara.

All of them dashed out of the hole in the wall of the silo. A black cloud billowed upward as an explosion burst out after them.

The rusty building blazed like a torch as the roof flew off, followed by the silo in entirety. Then, with a sudden gasp of wind, a giant flame rocketed into the sky.

Pablo and the others were hurled to the ground. They crawled quickly away from the fire, coughing and spitting out insects.

A hot wind swept over their sweat-stained faces. The orange and gold inferno blazed in their eyes. For a few moments, they all stared at the remains of the rusty tower.

Thora slowly stood. "Did we stop it?" she asked.

Pablo walked over to touch the silver fluid that had filled the pit. It had solidified into a hard metallic element and felt cold to the touch.

"Nothing's coming through here!" he said excitedly.

Mara nodded and smiled. "Yes," she said. "The *bazhargak* has been stopped. The trolls will not be able to enter our world from here."

Zak fell into a sitting position upon the ground. "Did that really just happen?" he said to no one in particular.

"Yep!" Louise said cheerily. She walked over to him and held out her hand. "You turned into a grizzly bear and scared away the big bad wolf."

Zak grinned. He took Louise's hand and stood, making sure to pretend the much smaller girl was helping him get to his feet. "You did pretty well yourself, kid," he told Louise.

"Really?" Louise asked, her eyes bright. "Did I really help?"

Thora smiled at Louise. "Really," she said, nodding her head. "You saved us."

Zak mussed up Louise's hair. "How's it feel to be a hero, kid?" he teased.

Louise smiled and giggled.

Pablo suddenly hooted, clapping Zak on the back. "That was awesome, man!" Pablo said. "I still can't believe you turned into a bear!"

"Speak for yourself," Zak said. "The way you were swinging those weapons, you looked like a Roman gladiator, or something."

Pablo laughed. Then he pointed at Thora proudly. "And what about her jar?" he said.

Zak smiled. "Yeah, that was pretty sweet, too," he admitted.

As Thora beamed with pride, Pablo noticed a glint of light flickering in her eyes. Then, for a moment, her eyes met his. Thora looked away and began to blush. Pablo shuffled his feet and looked at the ground.

Louise leaped between them, then started jumping up and down excitedly. "And the silver dress I wore!" she cried. "It was so pretty."

Zak just laughed. "You looked like . . . like . . ."

"Like Libra," finished Pablo. "Louise is a Libra. She holds the scales, balancing the sides, and turning the tide."

Louise smiled.

Mara nodded her head. "Without Louise's power of balance," she said, "your other powers would not have been enough. Each of you played an important part in this victory."

Mara stepped closer to stand between the four young heroes. "And I have a feeling you'll all play an important role in the battle to come."

The four companions were silent as they weighed the meaning of Mara's words. After a moment, Thora broke the silence. "You looked like Orion, Pablo," she said. "Like your last name."

Orion. O'Ryan. *That's what Mara said to me earlier*, thought Pablo. *She recognized me as Orion, the hunter.*

"Maybe Dr. Hoo was right," Pablo said. "Maybe *we* are the heroes from the stars!"

"We should go tell Dr. Hoo all about what happened," Thora suggested.

Mara smiled. "That's a great idea."

"And Dr. Hoo will know what we should do next," Mara added.

And with that, they all piled into the SUV and drove toward Dr. Hoo's house.

13

DOCTOR WHERE?

The SUV bounced along the rutted driveway. Its headlights waved up and down with each bump. Its horn honked cheerfully as they arrived outside Dr. Hoo's house. The shadows were shorter now, and more light seemed to shine through the trees.

Mara and the young heroes leaped out of the SUV. For a brief moment, they watched the tip of the fiery tower blaze in the distance like a bright orange finger pointing skyward.

Black smoke billowed from the tip and merged with the gray clouds overhead.

They rushed to the door and hurried inside. They were excited to share the good news with Dr. Hoo.

"Doctor!" Mara yelled. "The kids have done it! Where are you?"

They ran through the entire house yelling for the doctor, but their cries went unanswered. Their footsteps echoed through the halls as they rushed toward the library. Thora peeked around the corner of the door, fully expecting to see Dr. Hoo at the desk studying ancient tomes or astronomical texts.

Instead, the room lay dark and silent. At that moment, their lively voices dwindled into silence.

"He's not here," whispered Mara. "Why isn't he here?"

Just then, Thora spotted a long, dark cloak laying on the floor. She picked it up. "It's Dr. Hoo's cape," she said quietly.

As she lifted the cloak, she saw there was an object underneath. "Bryce's pocket knife?" Thora said. "What is this doing here . . . ?"

Pablo knelt down next to Thora. He pressed his fingers into a dark splotch upon the floor a few feet from where the cape lay. "Is this . . . blood?" he said.

Mara looked down at Pablo's fingers. "Yes," she said somberly.

Louise pointed at the wall above the pool of blood. "What does that word mean?" she asked.

Thora followed her finger. A word had been crudely carved into the wooden wall a few feet above the floor.

It read: *CROATOAN.*

Thora's heart sank. The word had been carved with a pocket knife. Bryce's knife. "What does *croatoan* mean?" Thora asked.

Tears began to well in Mara's eyes. She turned to face the window. "It means," she said, her voice quavering, "that Dr. Hoo has been kidnapped."

ABOUT THE AUTHOR

As a boy, MICHAEL DAHL persuaded his friends to celebrate the Norse gods associated with the days of the week. (Thursday was Thor's Day, his favorite!) Dahl has written the popular Library of Doom series, the Dragonblood books, and the Finnegan Zwake series. As a Norwegian lad from the Midwest, he believes in trolls.

About the Illustrator

BEN KOVAR was born in London. He trained in film and animation and spent several years as an animator and art director before moving into writing and illustrating fiction. He lives in an attic, likes moisture, and has a fear of sunlight and small children.

Notes on Dark Towers

"The gathool are a proud race. They see themselves as superior to all other forms of life and believe they alone should control the Earth and its resources. So it make sense that the trolls would rely on Dark Towers to travel to the surface — the bazharghak slices through anything in its path, leaving a swath of destruction in its wake."

— Tower of Terror, by Anthony Atwood Crake

Mr. Crake is a respected scholar on all things gathool, but he misses the point sometimes. Firstly, the trolls don't use Dark Towers because they're destructive. Rather, they rely on the towers because they are fast, direct, and provide shelter from the sun's harmful rays during the day.

Secondly, the drilling motion of the towers loosens the ground at the entry point, making the earth unstable for the less-than-sure-footed humans, giving the nimble trolls an advantage on rocky, jagged terrain.

Thirdly, the towers allow the gathool to create a direct path to the surface so that reinforcements can travel through the tunnel if backup is needed.

In order to have any chance at surviving a troll invasion, the bazharghak must be stopped from reaching the surface.

The Gathool Vocabulary

The gathool language doesn't have many words,
and the pronunciation is usually straightforward.
However, many gathool words have several meanings,
so translating the language is quite a challenge. Here
are some of the words I've managed to decipher...

BAZHARGAK (buh-SHAR-gok)—palace of night. A
bazhargak, or dark tower, is a gathool method of
transportation.

CROATOAN (croh-uh-TOH-uhn)—moving bridge.
Croatoans are used to move large numbers of trolls
between locations. A bazhargak is a type of croatoan
used by warriors.

DRAKHOOL (druh-KOOL)—trolls of the earth. The
gathool see the drakhool as their soft-hearted,
inferior siblings.

HROOM (har-OOM)—there is no standard definition
for this word. It sounds like a drum, and serves
as a rally cry for powerful troll leaders.

UZHK (OOSHK)—tranquil one. Uzhk is a drakhool,
and a friend of mine. He is one of the few trolls
who seems to enjoy the company of humans.

Benjamin K. Hoo

THE LAVA CROWN

"It doesn't make sense," Zak said. "Who could've kidnapped Dr. Hoo?"

Mara hesitated. "The *gathool* took him," she said. "He's being held by the trolls now."

Zak threw out his arms in frustration. "Then how can we get him back?!" he cried.

Mara took a step toward the wall. She pointed at the word etched into its surface. "Croatoan," she said. "It's a *gathool* word that means 'bridge to the underworld'."

Puzzled faces stared back at Mara. She opened her hands to take in all of the tower. "The *gathool* have marked this tower as a gateway to the their underground kingdom," she explained. "And we're going to use it to enter their world."

THE DARK TOWER HAS CRUMBLED,

TROLL HUNTERS

The Lava Crown

BY MICHAEL DAHL

BUT AN EVEN GREATER THREAT AWAITS...

Find websites and more books like this one at facthound.com.
Just type in the book ID: 9781434233080

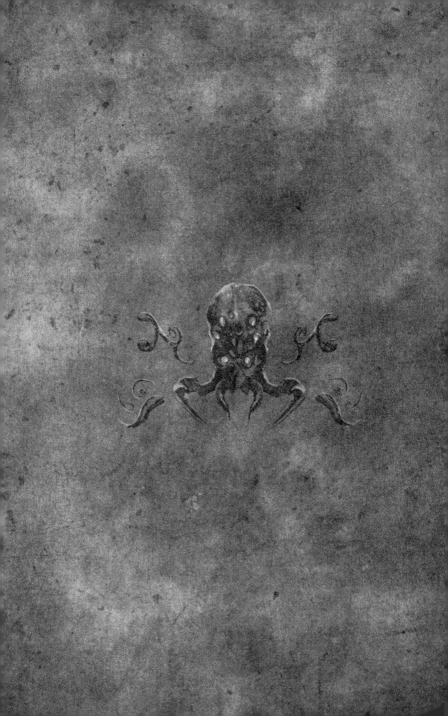